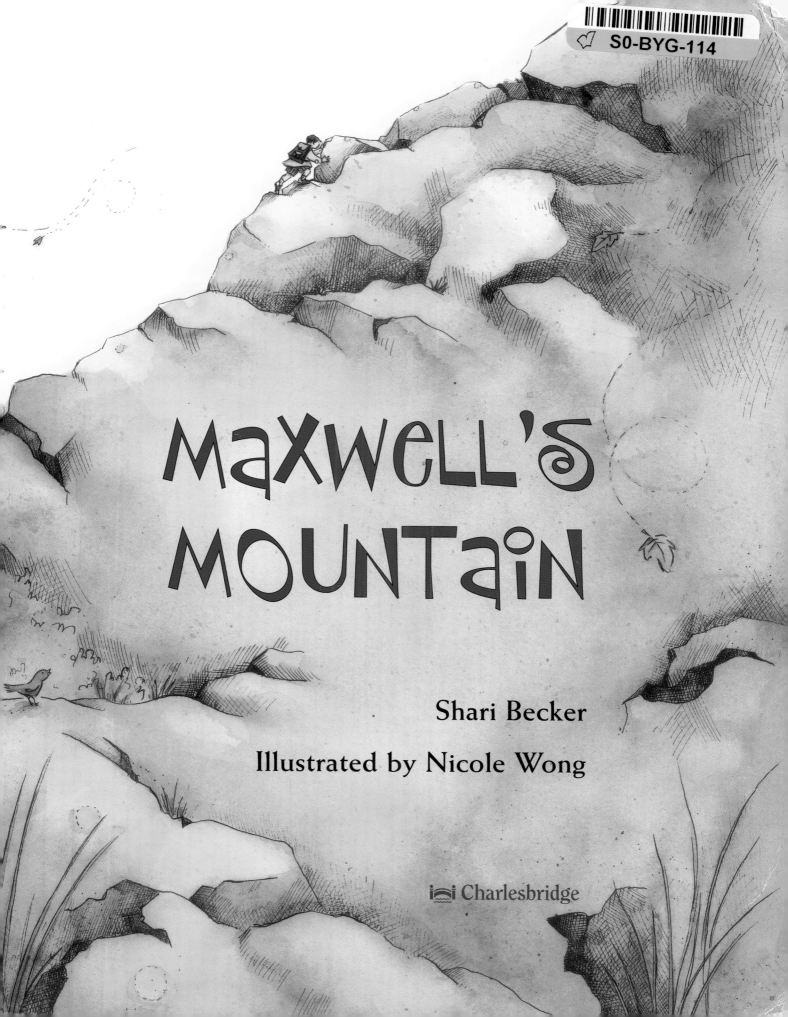

MaXWELL'S MOUNTaiN

Shari Becker

Illustrated by Nicole Wong

Charlesbridge

MAXWELL climbed to the top of the slide and pulled Harry, the soldier with the red beret, from his back pocket. Slides are always the best spot to check out a new park. He looked to the left and saw a swing set—typical. To the right he saw a sandbox—predictable. Directly ahead, a seesaw—common. He turned his head to look behind him, and then he saw it.

A mountain, standing tall. It was awesome. It was glorious. And it was big.

The mountain was made of yellow and brown boulders and had a wooden fence running around the top. It was a perfect lookout. Maxwell felt his feet pulling him toward the mountain.

"Come on, Harry," he whispered, and scrambled down the slide.

"Hold it, partner," said Maxwell's mom. "That hill is where the big kids play."

That's no hill. It's a mighty mountain, thought Maxwell, *and who says I'm not a big kid?*

At dinner Maxwell saw mountains everywhere.

But when Maxwell asked if he could climb,
his mom and dad agreed that he was too small.
   "To tackle a mountain, you've got to be a great
outdoorsman," said his dad.
   "Then I'll be a great outdoorsman," said Maxwell.

When his class visited the library the next day, Maxwell asked the librarian for all the books she had on mountain climbing. "I'm going to be an outdoorsman," he told her.

That night Maxwell looked through all his books and made a list.

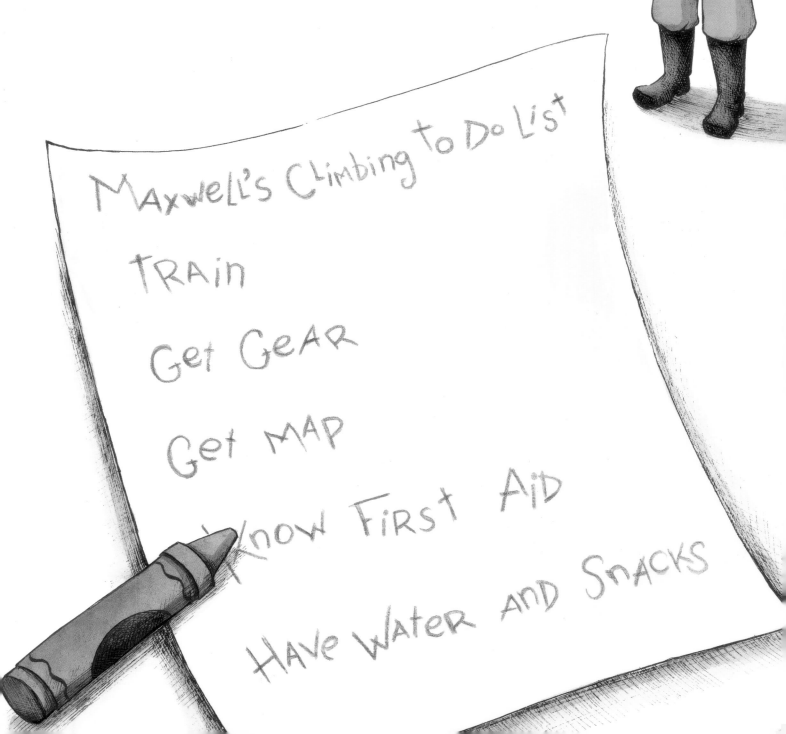

Maxwell's Climbing to Do List

TRAin

Get GEAR

Get MAP

Know First Aid

HAve WAter AnD SnAcks

Training was rigorous and hard. Every day
Maxwell and Harry climbed to the top of the
staircase four times. It was the tallest mountain
in the whole house. They practiced walking
up, scrambling up, and hopping up.

"What are you doing?" asked his mother.

"A true outdoorsman trains for an
adventure," he replied.

"I see," she said.

Maxwell and Harry drew a map of the
whole park. In the middle was the mountain.
"A true outdoorsman knows exactly where
he's going," said Maxwell to his mother.

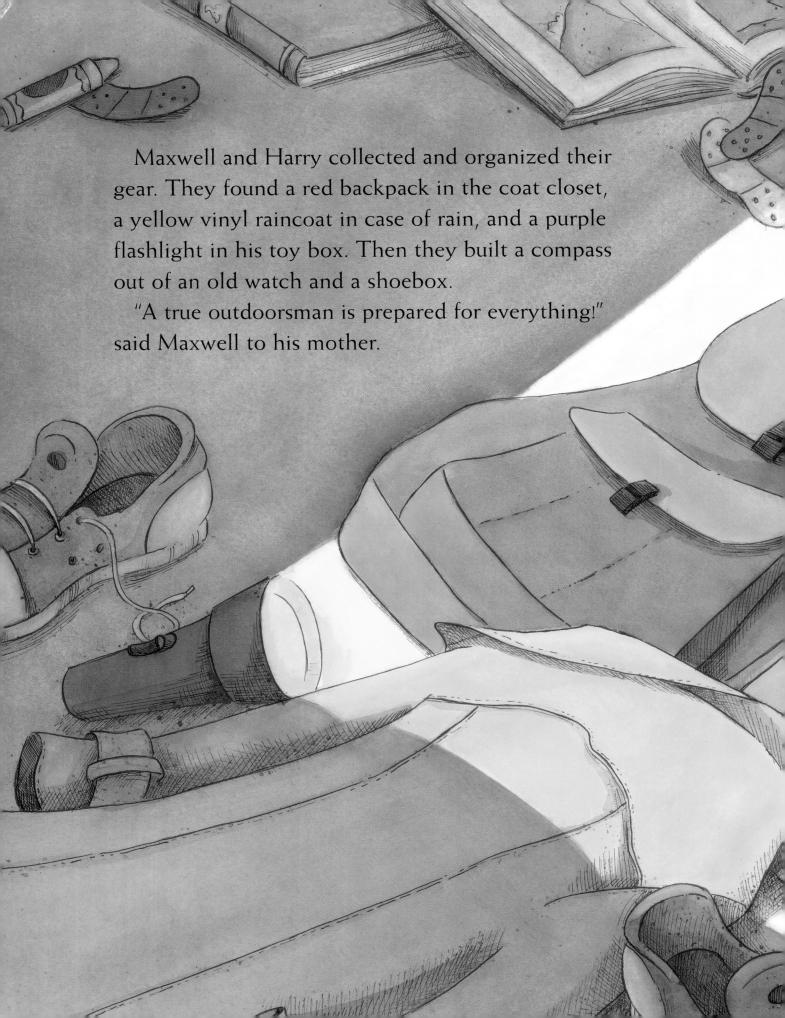

Maxwell and Harry collected and organized their gear. They found a red backpack in the coat closet, a yellow vinyl raincoat in case of rain, and a purple flashlight in his toy box. Then they built a compass out of an old watch and a shoebox.

"A true outdoorsman is prepared for everything!" said Maxwell to his mother.

But Maxwell wasn't done yet.
Maxwell and Harry put together a first-aid kit, too,
with 10 superhero Band-Aids and an old Superdog
pillowcase in case they needed a sling.

By now gear was sorted and lined up across Maxwell's bedroom floor, through the hallway, and down the stairs.

Maxwell's parents could barely walk around the house without tripping.

"Can I climb the mountain now?" he begged. "A true outdoorsman knows when he's ready, and I'm ready."

"Hmmm," said his mother. "Do you think you need assistant navigators?"

"I have Harry," replied Maxwell. "But you can watch."

"All right, Maxwell," replied his mother. "You can go. But don't forget—if he gets into trouble, a true outdoorsman uses his head."

Maxwell's Climbing to Do List

When they arrived at the foot of the mountain the next morning, Maxwell studied his map, pulled out his compass to make sure he and Harry were going in the right direction, then strained his neck and looked up to the top of the mountain. It was much bigger than he remembered. But from here he could see a trail making its way up the mountain. There were yellow dots leading the way.

"I'm off," he said.

And with that, Maxwell and Harry headed for the first yellow dot.

The bottom of the trail was made of little pebbles. "Easy peasy," said Maxwell.

Then the pebbles turned to larger stones.
The climb was just like his staircase at home.
"Piece of cake," he said to Harry. They took
a sip of their water and climbed on.

Soon the stones became rocks, and Maxwell
and Harry had to use their arms and legs to
scramble up. They stopped on a big rock and
snacked on an apple.

Harry was already tired, but they couldn't stop
now. "We must keep moving ahead, Harry," said
Maxwell. He looked at his compass to check
his direction.

Now Maxwell and Harry walked, climbed, and scrambled upward. At a cliff they ate their cookies and looked down at the sandbox, which was now smaller than Maxwell's hand. "Almost there, Harry," he said.

But the rocks were getting bigger. In fact they were more like boulders. Maxwell and Harry had to look down, not up, just to keep their footing.

Suddenly they could not climb anymore.
Maxwell looked up. The boulders ahead were
bigger than he was. He stood up on his tiptoes,
but he couldn't see over the tops. And where
were the yellow markings? He couldn't see one
anywhere. He looked at Harry. "I've lost the trail,"
he said.

Maxwell sat down and sighed. His map was no use, not here. His compass wasn't any help either. And what good was a water bottle now?
He scratched his head, feeling very lost.

And then he remembered. "When he's in trouble,
a true outdoorsman uses his head." His mom had
said it.

Maxwell began backing down exactly the way
he'd come. He slid backward down one boulder,
and then down the next. Going down was much
harder than going up. "A true outdoorsman is brave,
Harry," he said as he scrambled.

Finally he came to the last yellow dot he had passed.

He looked up, but he couldn't see another dot anywhere.

Maxwell stood on his tiptoes and looked around bushes and at the side of boulders. Finally, painted on a half-hidden stone, Maxwell saw a yellow dot.

"Where there is one, there's sure to be another, Harry," Maxwell said, and he started to climb again. This time he kept his head up. He spotted another yellow marker and another and another. "We're back on track, Harry," he said.

"We did it!" Maxwell cheered as he pulled himself over the last boulder before the top.

"Good job, Harry!" he said.

From the top he looked out. He could see the skyscrapers from the city, and he even thought he could see his roof. This really was a lookout. Spreading out his arms, Maxwell closed his eyes and took a deep breath.

When he opened his eyes, he saw it.

An ocean at the other end of town.
It was awesome. It was glorious.
And it was big.

To my husband, John: Thank you for your love, support, adventurous spirit, and passion for gear—S. B.

For Patrick, Thomas, and Catherine—N. W.

2007 First paperback edition
Text copyright © 2006 by Shari Becker
Illustrations copyright © 2006 by Nicole Wong

Published by Charlesbridge, 85 Main Street, Watertown, MA 02472 • (617) 926-0329
www.charlesbridge.com

Library of Congress Cataloging-in-Publication Data
Becker, Shari.
    Maxwell's mountain / Shari Becker; illustrated by Nicole Wong.
       p. cm.
    Summary: After preparing to be an outdoorsman, Maxwell sets out to climb the mountain in the park.
    ISBN 978-1-58089-047-2 (reinforced for library use)
    ISBN 978-1-58089-212-4 (softcover)
[1. Mountaineering—Fiction. 2. Parks—Fiction.] I. Wong, Nicole E., ill. II. Title.
PZ7.B381715Max 2006
[E]—dc22   2005013296

Printed in Singapore
(hc) 10 9 8 7 6 5 4 3 2
(sc) 10 9 8 7 6 5 4 3 2 1

Illustrations done in watercolor and ink on Fabriano paper
Display type set in P 22 Sniplash, designed by Terry Wüdenbachs, and text type set in Weiss.
Color separations by Chroma Graphics, Singapore
Printed and bound by Imago
Production supervision by Brian G. Walker
Designed by Susan Mallory Sherman